Dumb Luck

Adam Gibbs

Dumb Luck

Adam Gibbs

"The Edge… There is no honest way to explain
it because the only people who really know where
it is are the ones who have gone over."
Hunter S. Thompson (1966)

Part One

The vacation shaming started early.

It had started, in fact, at its earliest possible juncture, when I handed the paperwork to Joel, my boss.

"Miller, you never take a vacation!" he bellowed, incredulous, looking at the papers as if they were covered with ancient glyphs. His incredulity was well-founded: I had been with One World Travel for almost six years and never taken more than a day here and there. I was 29, single, childless, and lived alone. Where would I go? Why?

"I know, just figured it was finally time to get away," I shrugged.

"Get away," he chuckled, "Peoria's not so bad."

You're right, Joel, guess I'll stay.

"Yeah, I guess," I offered meekly, "Will it be OK?" I didn't need his permission, I was entitled to the days and they weren't until late September into October, more than two months away. Still, when approaching the boss, I tended to revert to my grade school self, asking the teacher if I could use the restroom.

"No…I don't think it should be a problem," he said, pausing just long enough to make me nervous. He was rubbing his mustache thoughtfully as he looked over the papers as if this were a major decision that might shut the agency down if he got it wrong.

"OK, then…thanks," I said, awkwardly turning to leave his office, happy he hadn't asked me where I was going because, in truth, I still didn't know.

I walked back to my desk, sat down, and took a deep breath. As a travel agent, I had every resource at my disposal to plan a trip. Deciding to take the trip, however, was more important to me than the destination.

The quiet solitude of my life had started to feel a lot like loneliness in recent weeks, and just up and leaving Peoria for a few days suddenly seemed like the best remedy. Traveling alone had previously struck me as sad and whenever I helped someone plan a trip on their own, I felt sympathy for them. The week before, however, I had helped a guy about my age plan a month hopping around India and Southeast Asia and found myself envying his freedom. Aside from the fact that he obviously wasn't hurting for money, I began to view this type of travel as a form of liberation. For some reason, I never really imagined myself taking such a trip until then. Why not, I figured. The isolation of my uneventful little life in Peoria suddenly felt stifling. After consulting the calendar for a few days, I determined to pick some days a few months down the line, satisfying the company's thirty-day requirement for vacation notices and giving me time to plan and save money. September 15 would be my last day, then I'd be off until October 9, using every available vacation day I'd stored up over the years.

"Hey, Owen, where are you going on your vacation?!" Nadia's always-cheery voice snapped me back to the reality outside my overactive mind.

"Huh?" I played for time.

"I was just talking to Joel, he says you're taking off in September. Where to?" She'd been at this job twice as long and always seemed to be in a good mood. How people like her maintained that emotional energy was beyond me.

"Oh, I, uh…I'm not really sure. Know a good travel agent?" I'd used some form of this lame joke a thousand times with family and friends. Nadia acted like it was the funniest thing she'd heard all week.

"You're too funny, Owen! How are we gonna replace you when you're gone?" Vacation shaming is a subtle art, sometimes.

"You'll get by," I offered, just wanting the conversation to end. When you live a long time alone, even these banal office rituals can quickly become trying.

"I'm just teasing you," she said, lightly patting my shoulder, "Enjoy your trip," she offered in parting, no doubt disappointed that juicy tidbits were not forthcoming.

Forcing myself to get back to work, I managed to be semi-productive for the remainder of the morning. At lunch, when I walked into the breakroom, I had the misfortune of finding myself alone, just for a moment, with Gary, the insufferable bore of the office who never shut up but never really said anything of interest. As I sat down and unpacked my lunchbox, vainly acting like I was the only one in the room, Gary looked up from his newspaper and traded his table for mine. The front page was occupied by headlines of the story dominating the news since the weekend.

"Some crazy shit down in Charlottesville, huh?" Gary observed, not even giving me the courtesy of eye contact. He was a talker, not a conversationalist.

"Yeah, awful stuff," I replied, wanting, like most sane people, to avoid talking about politics at work.

"Ah, I don't know, though. Some skinheads versus a bunch of fucking hippies who need to get jobs, not sure whose side I'd take," he quipped, obviously satisfied with his wit and ignoring the fact that it all happened on a weekend.

I offered a weak smile. The whole thing seemed bizarre and tragic but, then again, much of the fallout centered around the response of a former reality TV host who was suddenly president, so it was getting hard to tell what constituted bizarre or tragic anymore.

"Say, I hear you're leaving us in a few months," he changed course to the only topic that could have made me more uncomfortable at the moment.

"Yeah," I affirmed. Here it comes.

"Going to make a lot more work for the rest of us," he grinned, smugly.

I returned his grin with as much good humor as I could muster, feeling more every moment that this vacation would be such a welcome reprieve from all of this bullshit. Thankfully, a few other employees filed in at this moment, and Gary's attention span dictated that he move on to other unfortunate ears.

When the day mercifully ended, everyone knew I was going on vacation, but no one knew—or cared—where I was going. And I was right at the top of that list.

It was an odd feeling, planning a trip for myself instead of someone else. On the one hand, I was having my typical homebody weekend and enjoying it. On the other hand, I was hopping around the web on my laptop as I reclined in bed, growing more and more excited as ideas suffused my brain. Do I go abroad? Europe? Australia? Stay in the states? I'd always wanted to see the Pacific Northwest, an area of the country that seemed almost foreign to a kid whose idea of "going away to school" was the two-hour drive from Peoria to DeKalb.

Then it happened.

No blast of trumpets, no parting clouds; just an easy-to-miss link on an obscure accommodations site beckoning me to the most unoriginal of vacation destinations; flashy, touristy, and the last place anyone who knew me would expect me to go: Las Vegas. I smiled, chuckled to myself, and booked the trip.

The looks on their faces were priceless.

Over the next few weeks, every time a colleague tried to make idle small talk, they'd invariably ask about my upcoming vacation. When I matter-of-factly said I was going to Vegas, they looked at me as if I were green and had three heads. I tried not to smirk as I imagined them picturing Owen Miller, their mild-mannered, soft-spoken co-worker who loved books and writing, jetting off to

Sin City for a week of debauchery. The truth, I knew, was that I would be more of a spectator than a participant in such events, a postmodern Sal Paradise, shambling after, waiting for the pearl to be handed to me.

As August simmered to a close, I watched as a "once in a generation storm" swirled over the Gulf of Mexico and came ashore in Texas, bringing catastrophic flooding to dozens of cities, including Houston. Seeing the images of such disasters always forced me, at least for a moment, to imagine myself in such a situation. One night in early September, I thought I might find myself on the other end of this reflexive empathy.

It was Labor Day, and I'd refused an invitation from my best friend Alex to come over to his place for a cookout, partly due to prevailing social anxiety, but also because the weather forecast looked dicey. I promised him we'd get together the next week. That night, I was asleep on my couch with the TV on when, in my somnolence, a deep rumbling sound could be heard. I opened my eyes and drew in a breath upon hearing the sound, waking up quickly enough that I needed a moment to hone my concentration on what was happening. After a few more minutes, the sound grew in frequency and it was unmistakable that a storm was growling somewhere in the ever-closing distance.

Maybe I was thinking about Harvey's victims in Texas, or maybe I was just too tired, but I didn't get up, didn't turn the TV to The Weather Channel, didn't even go to the window to look outside. I stayed reclined on the couch, listening to the thunder reverberate around the city and watching the lightning momentarily join my TV screen in illuminating my dark living room. I heard the tornado sirens as I drifted off to sleep, feeling a strange peace come over me.

The next morning, I got ready for work and left my apartment, my first glance of outside since the previous afternoon. Later, I'd find out that there were funnel clouds spotted in Illinois and Indiana, and a tornado had touched down in Ohio. There were a few limbs down in Peoria, a few hundred people apparently lost power, but nothing too serious. I'd always loved being outside on mornings like this; the world looked mostly the same but felt just a little different, the air swept clean, the dim gray post-dawn light somehow luminous, the sense of possibility hanging just above the remnants of the storm. By the time I pulled into the parking lot at One World, I knew I wanted to write a poem for the first time in weeks.

At home, I had piles of notebooks containing over ten years of poetry, short stories, and many fragments and aborted efforts at both. I had, from time to time, at the suggestion of friends and family, submitted some of my work to be politely rejected by a handful of fine publications that wished me all the best in my future endeavors. Friends, relatives, colleagues, they all knew me as a writer but didn't know I hadn't completed a thought in many months and was starting to worry I just wasn't capable of finding my voice, or whatever they called it.

When I got to my desk, though, the muse was whispering to me at last, and I transcribed as best I could. I made do with One World Travel stationery, scribbling a few lines on the notepad we each had on our desks. When a stanza was starting to come together, I heard another voice. Not the muse, but Arthur, my favorite co-worker.

"Getting a lot done?" he quipped, glancing over the partition of my cubicle and at the verse growing, however slowly, on the paper.

"I'm trying," I smiled.

Arthur was in his early sixties and had retired from teaching English Literature at Illinois Central a few years back. If I'd stayed in Peoria and gone there instead of Northern Illinois, I often thought, I could have had him as a professor. He and his wife ran into financial trouble after the crash in 2008 and both went back to work. It was nice to have someone around the office who I could talk books with, and I even showed him some of my writing from time to time. It also helped that he was a nice guy. Like, Midwestern, salt-of-the-earth, "aw shucks" nice.

"Heard you're going to Vegas, a young man's town," he said, "Do you plan on doing any writing while you're there?"

He didn't say it like a teacher giving an assignment, but I knew part of him itched for me to hand him page upon page of poetry and prose to chew over.

"I bring my notebook with me every time I go on a trip," I hedged, having a sudden premonition that I'd while away the trip drinking in my hotel room and accomplishing little in the way of literary output.

"A change of venue will be good for you," he observed, a more insightful comment than he knew.

I glanced down at my notepad. "About the storm last night," I said, offering it up to him like a sacrifice. He gazed at it steadily.

The feeling of walking
Outside the morning after a storm,
When the world looks the same
But feels just a little different,

The air having been swept clean
For the next breath you gladly take in

I held my breath as if he were about to give me a grade of "incomplete."

"There's something here…perhaps you could explore the concept of changing perspectives at different times throughout one's life?"

Not a bad idea.

"Good idea, mind if I claim it as my own?"

He winked, handing the pad back to me.

"Good writers borrow. Great writers steal."

"Fight Club?"

It was Alex on the phone. It was the Monday after our Labor Day rain check (which I'd forgotten about).

"You got it."

He wasn't suggesting we pummel each other as a form of therapy. My oldest friend knew how to draw me out of my cave. It was our favorite movie from the first time we saw it as teenagers, partially because I always insisted Alex looked a bit like Ed Norton (he disagreed, but it had become our longest running joke). The main reason we loved the movie, though, was the psychological aspect of it, which we'd spent countless hours discussing.

We agreed on watching the movie at his apartment at 8 p.m. After driving a few minutes through town, I arrived at his building and was greeted at the door by Briane, his longtime girlfriend who was, by now, used to this male bonding ritual.

"Alex, Brad Pitt is here!" If he was Ed Norton, I was Brad Pitt. It was only fair.

Alex greeted me and the three of us sat down in the living room for the requisite catching up.

"What have you been up to, man?"

May as well hit him with it early, I figured.

"Actually, after this Friday, I'm on vacation for a few weeks."

"Really? Are you going anywhere?" Briane queried, her tone suggesting she wouldn't be at all surprised if I planned on just staying home.

"Yeah, I fly for Las Vegas on the 23rd and come back on October 2."

"Vegas?!" Alex blurted, with Briane looking agape.

"Yeah, I want to cut loose and have some fun. Why not?"

"No, it's a great idea, but it just doesn't seem like your kind of town."

"What's that mean?"

He looked uncomfortable for a fleeting moment,

then grinned, "You're Owen Miller, you play in Peoria."

I didn't want to smile, but I did. For decades, everyone from advertisers to politicians wanted to know if something "played in Peoria," because we had somehow acquired the mantle of Middle America's capital city (the alliteration probably helped, I thought).

We changed subjects to the ubiquitous topic of small talk, the weather. This time, though, it was in the headlines again. Another "once in a generation" storm was battering American shores, this time in Florida, and Alex and Briane observed that flying to Vegas at least would put me out of harm's way. As we talked, I couldn't help but notice the muted TV, tuned to one of the big news networks, was running a special about 9/11, as today was the anniversary. I thought about the passage of time and how this day used to stop us in our tracks every year, now it was to the point where it skated by like any other day until someone was filling out a form at the office and asked, "Is today the 11th?" There would be a moment of silent recognition where you both felt like someone should say something profound, but it quickly passed and the monotony resumed.

"OK, I guess I'll let you two get down to it, but my money's on Alex," Briane smirked, earning a playful middle finger from me. She gave Alex a kiss and me a hug, then adjourned to elsewhere in the apartment as Alex cued up the movie.

We had to have seen it fifty times or more down through the years, but it never got old to us. Even though we were just young enough to miss out on the demographic the movie focused on, I still got goosebumps when I heard Tyler Durden, patron saint of Generation X, give his speech about being history's middle children.

Enthralled, we watched with the rapt attention of first-time viewers, remarking only on a few favorite parts here and there. Alex may have resembled the Narrator, but I couldn't help but see myself in that character: an angst-ridden thirty-year-old boy trapped in life's relentless machine, an insomniac who just wanted to get some sleep but dreamed of changing his life. There's that part towards the end where Durden commends him for having the courage to "just run with it," after observing that most people in the world wish they could be someone else, and it always made me wonder. I didn't want to erase the debt record, but how could I run with it? How could I escape? Was there wisdom there or just movie magic? It was hard to tell the difference anymore. Almost every experience in my day-to-day life, I found, could be related to a movie, TV show, or even a commercial. Our emotions had been stylized, marketed, sold back to us for our own entertainment, a process that was reaching full speed right around the time we were born. I hated it, but I was it. I was it every time I tried to portray myself as a reclusive writer weighed down by genius instead of a guy on the verge of turning thirty who was still hiding from his own life. I was it every time I flatly characterized my co-workers as "Cheery Nadia," "Insufferable Gary," or even "Elderly Mentor Arthur." That line between the facts everyone could see and the fiction we told ourselves was being erased. Maybe, I thought, what I wanted in Vegas was oblivion, my own way of hitting bottom, my own private liberation.

The movie was drawing to a close. No lights were on and it had grown dark in the living room after the late summer sunset, a fitting setting while we watched the Narrator quietly take Marla Singer's hand as the skyline imploded. I wasn't sure if Alex felt it, but I got a chill watching the image of buildings collapsing on 9/11. As the credits started rolling, I found myself thinking back on my memories of that day.

"Great as ever, huh?"

I snapped back to the present.

"Yeah, thanks for suggesting it. I needed that."

We got up, embraced, and I said my goodbyes to him and Briane as she returned from the hallway. After driving back to my apartment, however, my mind went back to that cloudless morning sixteen years earlier.

It was a day like any other.

First-period science wasn't quite over yet, but we were done with our work and marking time until the bell rang. Another teacher appeared in the doorway beckoning ours to join him in the hallway. When she returned a few moments later, her voice was caught in her throat as she uttered, "Turn on the TV," to the student sitting behind me. He obliged and, suddenly, we were viewing the arresting spectacle of black smoke billowing from one of the Twin Towers, a strange pyre burning against the clear blue and glass of the Manhattan morning. "PLANE STRIKES WORLD TRADE CENTER," the banner on the screen proclaimed. Everyone on the air was still outwardly speculating (hoping?) that this was some horrific accident, but no one believed it. "We're gonna get to go to war with another country!" the student who had turned on the TV exclaimed, literally jumping for joy, his voice full of the sort of grim foresight and naïve glee that could only be possessed by an American teenager born in the late twentieth century.

By the time I made it down the hallway to my pre-algebra class, the second plane had hit the second tower, and any doubts as to what was happening had been removed. By the time the period had ended, the first tower had collapsed, the blackboard of the New York skyline was being erased, and the whole world had begun trying to solve for x.

After lunch, we had a teacher tell our social studies class about the tumultuous experience of growing up during Vietnam. Who knew how this morning's events would affect our generation, he said. The draft coming back had seemed far-fetched just a few hours before, but those planes had torn a hole in our reality and now anything seemed possible. The teacher said we weren't going to do any work in class today, that he was just going to turn off the lights in the classroom and give us time for reflection. I put my head down on my desk and closed my eyes, projecting myself into a future that seemed unreal yet frighteningly close. I imagined the draft being reinstituted. I imagined the hell of combat as much as I could bear. I imagined my name carved in black granite.

When I got home that afternoon, my dad mentioned that the FAA had grounded all civilian flights nationwide as I followed him out the door to our back patio. He mused about how many times we had been shooting hoops out here and stopped to watch the planes, tiny and distant in the sky above. We stood there in silence for a long moment, staring up into the emptiness and, though there were no planes to imagine myself looking down from, I still remember feeling very small.

This was the day: Friday, September 15th.

I was finishing up my last day before vacation, thoroughly enjoying the knowing glances from everyone in the office. I was the paroled inmate about to walk free, and though they were all smiling and wishing me well, the jealousy was palpable. Arthur was the only one I knew was genuinely happy for me. Toward the end of the day, I looked up from my desk and noticed him walking over.

"Just wanted to wish you well," he said with that magnanimous smile of his.

"Thanks, Arthur. I promise I'll get some writing done."

"Oh, that's alright. You can't force it. Just keep your eyes and mind open. Then, when it's your time, sing."

I felt like he was referencing some classic quote that I should know, but I was drawing a blank.

"Sing?" I said, hoping he would enlighten me.

"Do you know who the first poet in English was? The first one we know of, anyway?"

"You?"

He laughed harder than he had to, like when the president tells a joke.

"Lord, no! I'm not that old, though I feel like it sometimes."

"I give. Who was it?"

He pulled a chair over from an unoccupied adjacent cubicle and sat down, conspiratorial, as if he were about to tell me something subversive.

"There was an old English monk in the eighth century who told a story about a shepherd named Caedmon who tended to the animals at a monastery. One night, when the monks were feasting and singing songs around the fire, Caedmon left in shame, going out to sleep in the pasture with the animals because he was embarrassed for not knowing any songs. The story goes that he had a dream where he was visited by someone, an angel perhaps, who asked him to sing the beginning of created things. When he woke, he found he was inspired to compose verse and put it into song, and the rest is history."

I wasn't religious, but it certainly was poetic. I had to smile.

"Well, how could I not be inspired by that?"

We both stood up and he shook my hand.

"You're a good kid, Owen. Excuse me, a good young man. That song is inside you, just waiting to get out. When it's time, it'll happen."

I took a deep breath.

"Thanks again, Arthur. There's just one problem now."

"What problem?"

"I want you as my life coach," I smirked, his face turned blush red.

"No, you don't!"

"Hell yeah I do, come on, come to Vegas with me, we'll hit the casinos and strip clubs together, it'll be a blast."

We were both laughing loud enough by now to attract a few curious looks from other cubicles.

"You're too much, Owen. You have fun for both of us. How about that?"

"Deal," I said, finally letting go of our handshake.

A few minutes later, I was out the door and officially on vacation.

Actually, it was staycation first.

Before I flew for Vegas, I had a week to myself and Briane would surely smile at knowing I wasn't planning on going anywhere. I needed to make a grocery run Saturday to stock up but, other than that, I was planning on playing the reclusive writer for seven days.

After having pizza delivered Friday night for dinner, I drank the last two bottles of beer in my refrigerator—making a silent note to buy more—while I watched *Office Space*, the other touchstone film of my youth. I wondered if it said more about me or the society around me that my two favorite movies were focused on the relative problems of suburban malaise in modern America and the desire to escape a deadening of feeling that came with being a cog in the largest peacetime economic expansion in America's history.

Peter Gibbons was a rebel in a simpler, yet more profound way than Tyler Durden. He didn't want to reorder society by tearing down the machinery of hyper-capitalism. He just wanted to ignore the outside world, pull the plug on his alarm clock, roll over and go back to sleep. And yet he still incurred bafflement tinged with jealousy from his contemporaries. Vacation shaming wouldn't touch him, though; he just wasn't gonna go anymore.

I laughed at all the jokes I'd heard dozens of times and smiled as the closing credits started to roll. After channel surfing for a little while, I dozed off while watching a west coast MLB game. Around 3 a.m., I woke to an infomercial, yawned and stretched, and considered my next move, quietly ecstatic that I still had nowhere to be for over a week.

It was so quiet at this hour, it seemed a time conducive to writing. I got the crumpled piece of One World stationery with my most recent poem on it, a notebook and pen, and a couple of books off my shelf: Seamus Heaney and Sylvia Plath, grabbed at random in the dark. Copying the poem into my notebook, getting into the physical rhythm of writing, felt enabling and familiar, like remembering some special power I'd forgotten or left dormant for too long. A few new lines blossomed amongst my scribbles. Putting the new lines above the first ones suddenly had me feeling on the verge of completing the thought; those first lines after the storm made a better ending than a beginning. Arthur's advice to focus on the way our perspectives changed throughout life, an idea I stole with permission, is what tied it all together. I decided to title it *Perspective.*

There's no squaring that circle
That begins as a child when you
Wonder how something as small
As your thumb
Can eclipse the entire sun,
Which better minds have already
Assured you is so very big.

The lens through which you view
The world is in constant flux,
Its magnification changing
Since time immemorial,
Leaving certain mysteries
Just out of reach,
Lost in the middle distance,
Lingering like shadows at dusk.

Your memories are made and remade,
Rearranged every time a new truth
Conquers an old one,
The feeling of walking
Outside the morning after a storm,
When the world looks the same
But feels just a little different,
The air having been swept clean
For the next breath you gladly take in.

Each time you finish a poem, it's as if you've sharpened your entire life to a fine point, that it's all culminated in hearing a brief echo of perfection.

The volumes of Heaney and Plath hadn't been necessary to plumb for inspiration, but I reached out for Heaney regardless, Plath seemed too turbulent for this moment. For about an hour, I thumbed through the life and verse of a poet who had achieved the rare double of critical and popular acclaim. Somewhere between the rich Irish soil and the torment of history, I came upon his encounter with the spirit of James Joyce in *Station Island*, which sounded the same note as Arthur's lesson to me a few hours before.

You are fasted now, light-headed, dangerous.
Take off from here. And don't be so earnest,

so ready for the sackcloth and ashes.
Let go, let fly, forget.
You've listened long enough. Now strike your note.

(Seamus Heaney, "Station Island")

On the eve of a new phase of my life, the eve of a long journey, I felt, for the first time in so long, like the poet in me was awake, open to those small, miraculous moments that could change your life.

Late Saturday morning, I woke up and made my one intended trip of the week to get groceries. Normally, such trips were undertaken with expedience, wanting to get what I needed and get out with enough urgency that I often felt impatience bordering on anger while I waited in the checkout line, experiencing my own form of road rage as small talk was made, price checks were requested, and coupons were mined for. On this day, however, I was still infused with the spirit of Peter Gibbons from the previous evening's viewing. I didn't give a damn about much of anything, and so took my time idling through each aisle, filling my cart with everything I'd need for a week indoors in beautiful September.

When I had checked out and was pushing my cart toward the doors, the lottery machine, which I'd walked past a thousand times without a thought, caught my eye. I was getting ready to hit Vegas, right? I fed a $20 bill into the machine and got a handful of scratch-off tickets to take home with me. Once I had unloaded and put away my groceries, I sat down at my coffee table with that feeling that would keep casinos in business until kingdom come: that I was about to strike it rich. Using a quarter, I scratched off each of the tickets and found that I'd won a total of $12 between them. Subtracted from my $20 bet, that meant I'd lost $8, but I still felt like a winner, which probably meant it was a good thing I wasn't a big gambler. I had been saving up since July, accumulating a little over $400 in cash stowed away in a drawer of my writing desk. Those funds were designated for the casinos in Vegas. I told myself I would use that cash to gamble and no more, that I wasn't going to be that guy who made trips to the ATM and left town busted and broken. It wasn't fun to think about the end of a vacation, but I had been reminding myself that I'd eventually have to come back to Peoria and pick up my life where I left off, so I could stand to lose $400 but little more. But that same urge that brought a gambler to the table also, inevitably, had me thinking that maybe, just maybe, my $400 would turn into much more, that I would stumble into the kind of dumb luck often needed to change things for the better. I tried not to torture myself with thoughts of luxury items I'd purchase or more glamorous locales I could live in with a huge jackpot. I knew it was a longshot, but at least it was a shot I was taking. I should do that more often, I told myself.

For the next four days, I existed in a glorious state of torpor: I didn't shave, I took naps during the afternoons and stayed up all night reading and watching movies, and I had started accumulating a nice collection of empty beer bottles on the coffee table in front of a couch I rarely left.

It was late Wednesday night and I had my TV tuned to CNN, watching coverage of the third "once in a generation storm" this season to bring chaos and death to thousands of my fellow citizens. Hurricane Maria was devastating Puerto Rico and leaving most of the island flooded and in the dark, and once again I was drifting off to sleep on my couch, wondering how I had managed to avoid the catastrophe that seemed to be occurring with increasing frequency in America.

The knocking startled me.

My eyes snapped open with the thud-thud-thud at the front door of the apartment just a few feet from where I was curled up on the couch. Who the hell? I seriously considered just lying there in silence and waiting for whoever it was to go away. Reluctantly, though, I pulled myself up and staggered to the door, noticing that the sun was out and it was now Thursday, though I had no idea what time.

Opening the door, I found myself face to face with Alex, whose smile faded but quickly returned after laying eyes on me.

"Hey, man…you alright?"

"Huh?"

He looked me up and down.

"You look rough."

For the first time, I considered the state of me: I was wearing old basketball shorts and an undershirt, I had almost a week's worth of stubble, probably some bags under my eyes, and I had just woken up and was still adjusting to the light.

"I'm fine," I said, yawning and stretching, "Just enjoying the start of my vacation."

For a moment, I followed his glance past me to the empty beer bottles on the coffee table.

"I see that. Remind me when you leave for Vegas?"

"Saturday morning, 9:30."

"You need a ride? Save you some money on parking."

"Yeah, I'd appreciate that."

"Cool," he said, nodding his way into an awkward silence.

"So, what brings you here?"

He chuckled, no doubt amused by the fact it had taken us a full minute to get to this.

"Oh, I have the rest of the day off and thought maybe we could go somewhere for lunch."

We both laughed nervously. I did look a mess.

"I actually just woke up. Come on in."

I plopped back down on the couch and he took the recliner a few feet away.

"Been doing some drinking?"

"Just a little," I said, silently counting seven empty bottles on the table.

"Owen, is everything OK?"

His tone was decidedly more earnest.

"What do you mean? I'm fine."

"I just…worry about you, man. You're tucked away here all by yourself and have been for years.

I'm your best friend and I hardly see you anymore. I know you like the peace and quiet, but I don't know if this is the way you want to live. Is it?"

"Look," I sighed, "I know I don't get out much and yes, it gets lonely living like this, but that's why I'm taking this trip."

"You just don't seem yourself lately."

"What are you worried about, Alex?"

He looked around, as if physically searching for the words.

"I'm worried you're sliding back to the way you were at NIU."

Invoking my college experience was a sure way to get through to me. I'd spent a year and a half at Northern Illinois and it had made me miserable. I'd long had a feeling that everyone else my age seemed to have a plan, seemed to know what to do and when to do it, and I was just rudderless, trying to keep myself from drifting out into the deep.

"That was a long time ago. I've been working full time ever since, same job, same apartment. I've got it together, Alex," I spit the words out a little too aggressively, feeling my temper rise at the insinuation.

"I know," he countered, "But you're practically a recluse. If you don't get out into the world..."

"Then what?" I was annoyed, but genuinely curious as to where he was going with this.

"I don't know. That's probably a question you have to answer."

I scoffed and, for some reason, thought of a memory from long ago.

"When we were freshmen in high school, remember how the guidance counselors would come around to the homerooms and tell us how important college was? That we better start thinking about it right then?

"Sure."

"Well, when the counselor came to my room, he asked for a show of hands. How many of you know you definitely want to go to college? There were about two dozen kids in that room and everyone's hand went up except mine. I could feel all the eyes settle on me for a moment before he said something about how it was great that 'most' of us were sure. I just wasn't. I went because I didn't know what else I supposed to do. It was always going to end the way it did…and I'm always grateful for the help you gave me."

He forced an appreciative smile. I'd gone back for my sophomore year but missed a lot of classes, wasn't sleeping much, and couldn't motivate myself to do much of anything but stay in my room and drink. I managed to get to Christmas break, but faced a dilemma. My parents' marriage had been breaking up all through high school and the divorce had been finalized that previous summer. My dad had been in a relationship with another woman for about a year and she'd convinced him to move with her back to Modesto, California, where'd she'd grown up. It forced them to sell the house I'd grown up in and my mom had relocated to Chicago. Suddenly, I was thinking about coming home to Peoria but had no home to go to. I spent the first few days with my mom in Chicago, but things were strained. When your parents are divorced, you feel this toxic mixture of sadness and frustration. We went through the motions of Christmas, but I just wanted to get away from the divorce, from school, from everything. On Christmas night, I drove back to Peoria and turned up at Alex's old apartment, before he was living with Briane. I looked and felt like shit and told him I needed a place to crash. I spent that week between Christmas and New Year's sleeping a lot, drinking even more, and convincing myself that I wasn't going back to De Kalb when school started up again.

"Is there anything I can do to help you now, Owen?"

There wasn't. Besides, he'd done enough when he put me on to a landlord that had an apartment for rent and a cousin of his who worked at One World and got me in there.

"No, man. I promise you I'm fine, I'm just taking this time to rest and recharge, then I'll enjoy a week in Vegas having fun. It's all good."

"What about after that?"

"I'm on vacation," I sighed again, "I'm not thinking about the after."

He looked disappointed.

"Owen, what the hell are you doing with your life? What are you going to do?"

I didn't have an answer for him. I still couldn't raise my hand, and, for the first time, I considered the possibility that this could be selfish. When all else fails, liken what you're going through to a movie, right?

"I don't know, man. You ever feel like your life is a movie where nothing much happens?"

"No," he said, looking confused.

"I just..." I trailed off, not having the words. Alex suddenly looked conciliatory.

"It's OK, man. Sorry to bust you up like this, I just worry about you."

"You mentioned that," I quipped, earning a grudging smile in return.

"I'll get going. Look, you still have all day tomorrow before you fly out. Get out and do something, anything, take a walk, whatever. OK?"

Maybe he had a point. I'd had my stretch of lethargy, so perhaps it would do me good to breathe some Midwestern air before flying out to Vegas.

"OK. Will do," I nodded as we both stood up and walked toward the door. Before he left, he turned back with one more request.

"Oh, Owen, one more thing."

"Yeah?"

"Shave."

For my last full day before Vegas, I decided to pay a visit to a site I'd been meaning to see again for years. The Abraham Lincoln Presidential Library and Museum was little more than an hour down I-155 in Springfield. I'd been there in sixth grade on a class field trip and it was one of my fondest school memories. I was already developing an interest in history, an interest this trip helped to fuel, and it was one of the first times I grasped that those men in the marble statues were actually flesh-and-blood humans. Another memory that made me smile was from the end of that trip; Alex and I had each purchased cans of Coke from vending machines, and we spent the bus ride back ducking for cover behind the seat in front of us and sipping the sugary drinks as if we were getting away with drinking beers and failing to stifle our laughter.

It would be great, I thought on the drive down, to walk through this museum as an adult who better understood the history within, even though the legacy of Lincoln and the Civil War was still being disputed.

Once I walked through the doors, a quick scan of the patrons revealed no less than two groups of schoolkids being guided through on field trips by vigilant teachers and chaperones trying to impart some culture while keeping the chatting and roughhousing to a minimum. I was stunned simply to acknowledge the mathematical truth that that trip I'd been on had been more than a decade and a half ago. As I drifted through the exhibits, viewing the artifacts and wax figures of Lincoln and his contemporaries, it occurred to me for the first time that my own contemporaries may view my Vegas getaway as a desperate attempt to hang onto my youth, one last fling with my 20's before the beginning of that new decade that was supposed to herald the fullness of one's adulthood, whatever that meant. Maybe that was the reason for Alex's questions; he thought the coming milestone was triggering some sort of life crisis for me. Was he right?

I ended my trip to the hallowed past by sitting through a presentation called "Ghosts of the Library," where a live historian interacts with holographic projections of Lincoln and other images from his life and times. It bordered on hokey at times, even if the technology was impressive. But there was an audible gasp from the patrons when Lincoln's image first appeared and, though I kept silent, I had to admit that the visage of the great man, however illusory, gave me goosebumps. As the presentation ended, our historian "revealed" himself to be the ghost of a Union soldier killed in the war before subtly switching places with his holographic self and fading into the mists of time.

Driving home in the twilight, I kept thinking of that moment when it felt as if Lincoln's ghost had really appeared and made eye contact with me. I found it impossible not compare the past and present, wondering what Lincoln would think of this particular moment in the nation's history. From time to time, one would even hear feverish talk of another civil war looming. It was talk I shrugged off, not because I didn't think it was possible, but because I knew in my bones that our generation hadn't the gumption for anything so drastic. We'd just keep using poor spelling and grammar to insult each other on social media until we all just went out of our fucking minds. America had always been a big country with a raucous public life, but seldom, I guessed, had it ever been as tawdry and small as it had become in recent years.

Pulling back into my apartment complex, I had to tell myself to snap out of it. I needed to get away, and tomorrow it was time to make my escape.

My bags were packed and sitting on the couch. I'd had a quick breakfast of cereal and juice as the sun was rising, then took a few minutes to stretch out on my bed once I was dressed. Gently closing my eyes, I took long, deep breaths, a sort of meditation to prepare myself for the hustle and anxiety that would come with the next twelve hours of travel.

As usual, Alex arrived right on time. I had my bags in hand and was heading out my front door before he'd even finished parking. After throwing my stuff in the back seat, I hopped in and found him in a much better mood than when we'd last seen each other. The tension of a few days before was gone and we set out for Midway, O'Hare's slightly less hectic neighbor. After pleasantries, I told him about the previous day's excursion.

"Took your advice and got out yesterday," I started.

"Oh yeah?" he was already sounding pleased.

"Yeah, I actually went to the Lincoln Museum in Springfield, brought back a lot of good memories of our field trip."

His smile mirrored mine.

"Sipping our beers on the bus," he chuckled.

"The most rebellious thing we ever did in school," I confessed.

"That's good, man. I'm glad you went."

I feared he might revisit our heart-to-heart from Thursday, but he quickly changed the subject as we listened to sports talk radio from Chicago engage in the annual September fretting over the Bears and their slow start.

"You gonna bet some money on the Bears tomorrow?"

"They're playing Pittsburgh," I observed.

"Yeah, but you're in Vegas, might as well go for it."

"I'll pass," I said, ending our tongue-in-cheek debate. The truth was I'd researched sports betting online in the last few weeks and found the whole apparatus to be confusing and even intimidating. I felt the same way when I looked into table games. I wasn't destined to be a high roller.

When we pulled up to the curb at Midway, I gathered my shoulder bag and wheeled my suitcase around from the back of Alex's car to say my goodbyes. I reached in through the open passenger window and shook his outstretched hand.

"Thanks, buddy."

"Go have some fun," he said, leaving it at that.

As I walked towards check-in, I found myself grateful that he'd kept things light and didn't revisit any of the history we'd touched on forty-eight hours before.

After getting my boarding pass printed, checking my bag, and passing through security, I power-walked my way through the terminal and found the waiting area by the gate where my flight would be boarding. Sitting down, I exhaled a huge breath as if I'd been up against the clock when, in reality, I still had at least half an hour before boarding began. I'd long had this all-consuming fear of being late and I was never really sure where it came from. What I knew was that it was responsible for the only recurring dream I'd had in my life; over the last ten years or so, I'd constantly found myself wandering the halls of my old high school between classes, having lost my schedule, filled with panic and embarrassment as the day kept moving and I hadn't the slightest clue what to do. For reasons I couldn't fathom, the simple act of making this flight was feeling like an ordeal for me.

Once the calls started being made, I lined up with my soon-to-be fellow passengers, silently hoping I wouldn't get stuck sitting next to someone like Cheery Nadia or Insufferable Gary. I just wanted to zonk out as we reached our cruising altitude and not come to until we were ready to land.

The plane had five seats per row, three on the right side of the aisle and a pair on the left side, one of which I settled into by the window looking out onto the wing. The seat next to me remained unoccupied for a few minutes as people filed past. Finally, an older lady with white hair and an enormous carry-on bag sat down next to me. As we taxied onto the runway and prepared for takeoff, she pulled out a dog-eared paperback and started reading intently. We hadn't said a word.

At last, I felt the plane lurch forward as we began gathering speed. I'd flown about a dozen times before, but the moments between ignition and take off always filled me with a vague sense of dread. I tried to relax, but the more I did the more I could feel the tension: the changing pressure on my head and chest, the crackling in my ears, the tension vibrating up from the floor and through my feet, through the armrests and down to my fingers, those twin sensations of speed and motion that were proof of life.

The wheels were up, and the sprawl of Chicago shrank and shrank until it disappeared beneath us.

My head was against the window as I drifted in and out of sleep. Periodically, I'd hear an electronic tone over the PA or the drone of the engines. At an indeterminate point, a female voice cut through the relative silence and informed me that snack and beverage service would be beginning shortly. I gathered myself and noticed the lady next to me was still engrossed in her book. I stayed awake as the carts came to a stop next to us. She asked for a bottle of water and some peanuts. My stomach was feeling a bit uneasy, so I got ginger ale and a package of cookies. Sipping the drink and nibbling on the tiny cookies helped calm my growling stomach and I started to drift back off with the empty cup and wrapper still on my tray table in front of me.

The next time I came to, a flight attendant was approaching to collect trash. When she came to our row, my silent neighbor politely took the wrapper-filled cup from me and placed it in the attendant's bag along with hers. It was our only interaction on the entire flight. Soon, the pressure began to change again, the tension started to mount and continued until I felt the jolt that came with the wheels screeching down on the runway at McCarran International Airport in Las Vegas, Nevada.

Part Two

The tension didn't subside.

Even though I was safely on the ground at my destination, that looming feeling of worry still spread over me. From slowly filtering off the plane to claiming my bag to the Uber ride to the hotel, the feeling that I was about to be late or miss something persisted. When my driver dropped me off in front of the Mandalay Bay, I felt like I was back home and returning from the grocery store: I just wanted to get to my room and close the door as soon as possible.

The woman at the front desk who checked me in was a Cheery Nadia type, so happy to see me and insistent that I enjoy my stay. I smiled tensely and then reproached myself as I wheeled my luggage toward the elevators. I was on vacation, it was time to relax and enjoy the ride.

I took an elevator up to the thirty-first floor and found my room about halfway down a long hallway. Upon entering, my first order of business was to shed my baggage and flop down on the bed, exhaling and reassuring myself I'd made it. I hadn't done a damn thing yet, but for some reason just lying on the bed and taking some deep breaths made me feel victorious.

When I got back to my feet, I finally walked over to the window and inspected the view, a hotel rite of passage. Searching my memory, I decided this was the highest floor I'd ever stayed on in a hotel, so it would be a new experience to have such a perch. There was a large parking lot down below next to the hotel, then the Strip, which looked almost ordinary in the daylight; the bright signs and gaudy architecture making it look like a carnival midway waiting for nightfall. Beyond the Strip, there was a large open lot fenced in with a staging area that looked like it might be for a concert. Turning away from the window, I sized up my room. As Vegas hotel suites go, I knew it was pretty standard, but I had to admit that, for me, it was palatial, as big as my apartment and probably better furnished.

I decided that I was overdue for a full meal after what already felt like a day of traveling. There wasn't much difference between the duration of my flight and the time change between Chicago and Vegas, so I had this weird sensation that time had barely moved when I looked down at my watch. I took the elevator down to the ground floor and ghosted my way through the lobby, which was still teeming with people, finally emerging into the bright sunshine and the wool blanket that was the desert air in late September. It wasn't oppressively hot like I had feared, but it certainly was a change from the humidity I was used to in Peoria.

Walking across the street from the hotel, I saw signs advertising the Route 91 Harvest Festival around the empty lot, some of them showing a lineup of country music artists set to perform the next weekend. I wasn't really into country music, so it didn't interest me much, and I could practically see the entire stage from my hotel room window. As I made my way down the sidewalk, I finally settled on a smaller restaurant that looked to be a family-run place. It being between lunch and dinner time, there wasn't much of a crowd. I enjoyed a large hamburger and steak fries washed down with a tall glass of ice water. My stomach was empty enough that a greasy, heavy meal was ill-advised, but I was famished.

After emerging from my food coma, I walked a few more blocks before crossing the street and turning back towards Mandalay. There were casinos wherever you looked, so I told myself I'd explore more later in the week. For the time being, I headed to the casino in my own hotel and spent the first few dollars out of my "gambling fund" on slots, the table games still being too intimidating for a novice. I watched as my total fluctuated a few dollars up and down amid the din of electronic melodies. At my third machine, my first play resulted in a dizzying flash of lights on the screen and a celebratory tune from the speakers that reminded me of the ones I'd heard while playing Nintendo as a kid. As my total started climbing, I looked up at the key of symbols on the top of the machine but couldn't make much sense of it. A few people at other machines in my row looked over as the total finally stopped near a hundred bucks, putting me up about fifty from where I'd started.

"Nice job!" an older lady next to me observed as if there were any skill involved. I just laughed and nodded in acknowledgment. I decided it was a good time to cash out for the day, so I took my betting slip to a machine and walked away with just enough money to reimburse me for the meal I'd eaten earlier.

On a crowded elevator back up to my room, I suddenly felt tired. It was mid-afternoon, but the big meal, the heat, the travel, and the time change all conspired to make my body feel like it was almost time to crash. Tomorrow was an NFL Sunday, so I told myself I'd watch the Bears/Steelers game in one of the Mandalay's bar areas. Back in the room, I changed to a pair of gym shorts and stretched out on the bed, eventually falling asleep around sundown with the TV on.

I woke up in the middle of the night. Slowly, my eyes opened in the dark, seeing the familiar blue strobe of the TV's light against the wall. For just a moment, I panicked. It had been so long since I'd woken up in a hotel that the strange surroundings momentarily had me at a loss. After bolting upright in bed, I felt relieved to remember where—and why—I had been sleeping.

The alarm clock glowed from the nightstand. It was 4:24 a.m. I let out a long yawn and swung my legs over the side of the bed, my eyes finally adjusting to the contrast between the night and the TV's glare. My internal clock was way off due to the time change, but I decided if ever there were a time and place that internal clocks shouldn't matter, this was it. I left the TV on as a kind of nightlight as I made my way to the bathroom and climbed in for a long, hot shower, letting the steam work its wonders to wake me up.

Feeling refreshed and like my body had finally recovered from the travel, I picked through the small pile of promotional brochures and hotel information on the desk that was set against the wall. On a small card from Mandalay, I found the details about room service and the accompanying costs. In the last twenty-four hours, I'd consumed no more than a burger and fries, a glass of water, and some tiny airline cookies along with a ginger ale. Studying the card as I dialed, I called and ordered a full breakfast along with a newspaper, to be delivered, the kindly voice said, within the hour.

The sky was starting to lighten. I walked over to a semi-comfortable armchair by a table near the window and stared out as the city built for night slowly lost its luster with the coming of day. It was an odd feeling; though I was just starting my day and vacation, I saw the city as a sort of vampire, retreating to dark, cool places until the sun settled back down. Just before six, there was a soft knock at the door. When I answered, a young guy with a cart dutifully handed me a tray containing a plate of pancakes, eggs, and toast, along with a glass of orange juice and the Sunday edition of the Las Vegas Review-Journal. Sitting back at the small table, I took my time eating the food as I perused the paper and watched the sunrise. In the sports section, I couldn't help but glance at the NFL odds and notice that the Bears were, naturally, a home underdog to the Steelers.

It was a game day, so I pulled on my navy blue Bears t-shirt and headed down in the elevator a few minutes past kickoff. There was a bar area near where I entered the casino and seemingly a million flat screens showing every NFL game and sporting event under the sun. After studying the dizzying mosaic for a minute, I located a screen showing the game from Chicago and found a seat at the not-too-crowded bar. As the first quarter wore on, more people streamed in and the reactions became louder and more animated as a lot of money was undoubtedly riding on these games. The Bears were playing surprisingly well and had the lead as I sipped a cold beer and noticed a guy slide into the seat next to me; fortyish, tan, well-coiffed black hair, he looked a bit like an evening news anchor just come in from a round of golf as he studied the game silently for a few plays.

"How's it going so far?" It took a moment for me to register the question could only be directed at me.

"Well, they haven't put Trubisky in yet," I shrugged.

He broke into a smile.

"That's good," he glanced at my t-shirt, "Always good to bump into Chicago guys around here. I'm David…" We shook hands.

"Owen Miller," I said, then adding, "From Peoria."

"Peoria?!" he beamed, "My old buddy Mike Gillan lives there, you know him?"

Peoria may have been small compared to Chicago, but people from the latter were always acting like the former was a village where everyone knew everyone and we didn't lock our doors. "No," I said, after the requisite thoughtful pause, "Doesn't ring a bell."

"What brings you out?" he asked, moving on.

"Vacation, first full day in town."

"No better town for it, man. How you doing so far?"

I almost responded immediately before realizing that, in Vegas, that question had a different context altogether.

"Oh, I'm up about fifty," I said trying to sound casual.

"Goddamn, atta boy!" he blurted, impressed, and smacking me on the back like an old buddy.

"You live out here?" I made my first attempt at small talk in a long time.

"Nah, I'm always on the move, but I spend a lot of time out here."

"What do you do?"

"Dabble in a few things," he said, cryptically, not taking his eyes off the screen. "What about you?

"I work for a travel agency in Peoria."

"Yeah?" he said, raising his eyebrows and briefly turning to face me. "Probably got this trip for next to nothing?"

"Yeah, not too bad," I said, as if I traveled all the time.

"How much you got on the Bears?" he wondered, changing the subject as his mixed drink arrived.

"Ah, I don't bet the games, not my thing," I said, unsure of how he'd react.

"Really?" he said, seeming curious for a moment before nodding in approval. "A true fan," he concluded, patting me on the back again. "I usually take the points when they're an underdog. I'm sure Pittsburgh will have a better year, but it's early, so I took a flyer and put it all on the Bears to win."

It dawned on me that he may well have taken my saying I was up fifty to mean fifty thousand instead of fifty bucks. I wondered how much "putting it all" meant.

"Looking good for you so far," I observed.

"Yeah, so far," he responded with the weariness of a seasoned gambler.

His apprehension proved prophetic, as the Steelers mounted a comeback in the second half and forced overtime, with the two of us getting more emotionally involved as the game wore on.

When Jordan Howard ripped off a 19-yard game-winning touchdown run, I cheered and started to jump out of my seat but couldn't, as David had thrown his arm around me and let out a primal yell that about drowned out the rest of the screaming patrons.

"Oh, that's what it's all about!" he exhaled, finally starting to calm down. I watched his chest almost heaving, studying him like some alien creature next to me. NFL Sundays in Vegas were truly a different ballgame, I told myself.

We discussed the game for another minute before he threw down some money on the bar and looked to be ready to leave.

"Good talking football with you," he said.

"Yeah, it was fun," I responded, offering another handshake. As he accepted it, it seemed a thought jumped into his mind.

"You know what? Here…" he pulled his wallet back out and quickly removed a white business card, which he handed me. It had some kind of logo with a "DB" imprinted on it and simply said "David Blake" beneath it, nothing more. I studied it curiously.

"If you're still in town Saturday night, come by my suite at The Mirage, big party, always room for a Chicago guy," he said, restoring me to Windy City status.

"OK," I stalled, "What do I…"

"Just stop by the front desk and ask for me, they'll help you out. Come live it up with us, it's your vacation, right?" It all sounded so reasonable coming from him, but I suddenly found myself worrying I was being sucked into some elaborate con. This was the town for that, right?

"I guess so, I'll try to stop by," I offered as if I was meeting some foreign dignitary that same hour.

"Cool. Later." With that casual goodbye, I watched David Blake saunter off through the now-crowded casino. I'd made a friend—sort of—in Vegas. But I wasn't sure how to feel about it just yet, so I sat back down and ordered another beer.

I spent a few hours gambling after the game, losing about twenty bucks, then went back up and ordered more room service. As I sat eating at the window again, I laid David's business card on the table and glanced at it between bites, each time thinking up some awful new scenario, grim variations of a narrative that saw me being beaten and robbed or even killed because I was dumb enough to walk into some strange Vegas hotel suite on the invitation of a degenerate gambler. Maybe I was crazy? After all, nothing that interesting would ever happen to Owen Miller, would it? I wasn't destined to be Got Mugged in Vegas Guy in anyone else's movie. I told myself to dismiss the paranoia and consider that this just might be a party and a fun time and a great story to tell someday. Maybe I'd go, but I still had a week to talk myself out of it, and I knew I'd try.

What happened next was unplanned but, in hindsight, probably inevitable.

It was Monday and I was gambling at Mandalay. It was Tuesday and I wasn't sleeping much. It was Wednesday and I was raiding the mini-bar in my room, getting drunk, and wandering down the Strip past all the temptations of the city with nothing more than a vague curiosity. It was Thursday and I hadn't shaved all week, looked like hell, somehow having slipped back into that reclusive state I was in for a few days back home before Alex snapped me out of it. Each night I'd drank in my room and each morning I'd ordered breakfast and sat there silently eating and gazing out the window as the TV droned on. It was Thursday night and I was back in the bar watching the Bears play like shit against the Packers and David was nowhere to be found. It was early Friday morning and I shuffled back up to my room, the hotel now dotted with straw cowboy hats atop the heads of people in town for the festival I told myself I'd watch from my room.

I hadn't written a word all week and had no ideas, there was no twenty-first century *On the Road* in the works, no matter how feverishly I tried to imagine David, a guy I'd met once, as my Dean Moriarty. My notebook sat untouched in my shoulder bag on the desk. Arthur was going to be so disappointed. My story was far from a page-turner: a few years of school here, a few years of a job there, and soon I'd be waking up to thirty, no epiphanies, no revelations, no pearls handed to me.

Time had seemed to blur, not because I was moving so fast but because I was refusing to move with it. I'd let myself fall behind again and there was nothing poetic about it; it was dizzying and depressing. Maybe there was no point to it all. Maybe you just slog through this world and try not to be driven to madness by what's happening around you. I think Hunter Thompson had a phrase for it.

"Another freak in the freak kingdom."

On Friday night, I finally shaved and got up the courage to go for a walk down the Strip looking for The Mirage. I had finally convinced myself to go to the party the next night and wanted to walk the route. The Mirage was down towards the other end of the Strip, but it wasn't a bad walk in the warm, dry evening air. On my way back to Mandalay, I could hear the festival was in full swing and the area was crawling with people. Before crossing the street back to the hotel, I stood outside the barricades and listened to the roar of thousands of people cheering over the music. Standing shoulder to shoulder in a crowd and unable to hear myself just didn't sound fun, as much as I might have wanted it to. Later, I told myself I'd watch this festival of lights and muffled sounds through the glass of my room window. As I walked across the street to the hotel, I wondered how everyone back at One World was envisioning my trip and laughed at the distance between their fantasies and my reality.

I decided to get a drink in the same part of the casino where I'd watched the games and it was packed. After ten minutes, I finally snagged a seat at one of the bars. The TV's were all on again and cheers or jeers would go up every time something would happen in the baseball games, the pressure being greater in this final week of the regular season. One of the TV's had CNN on and I glanced up at it in time to see a muted report on what was happening in Afghanistan, a war so distant as to be practically invisible. For a moment, I thought about 9/11 and watching *Fight Club* with Alex back in Peoria, but my thoughts were quickly interrupted by a loud commotion behind me.

As I whirled around in my seat, a stampede of college-aged kids came through the bar area. There was a dozen of them screaming giddily, laughing too loudly, shitfaced on a Friday night in Vegas. One of the guys, I noticed, was wearing the head to a polar bear costume and nobody seemed puzzled by this. As my glance followed this masked mammal, I felt a slap on my shoulder and was soon face-to-face with the culprit, a happy young brunette who practically screamed in my face, "Get lit, motherfuckers!"

I tried to smile at the silliness of it all but could only manage a smirk as most of the patrons carried on, unfazed. Turning back to the screens, the war continued on mute, the gamblers cheered as a double was laced down the third base line, and I sipped my beer and considered how strange it was to be alive right now.

I hadn't been to a party in years, so I didn't know what time to show up. David hadn't exactly given me details. Trying on a few different shirts, I felt like a nervous teenager getting ready for his first date, wondering why I hadn't outgrown this social anxiety like seemingly everyone else I knew. A little after ten, I slid David's business card into my jeans pocket and headed out to walk the route I'd scouted the night before.

Walking across the street near the hotel, I caught my eye on something I never envisioned in Las Vegas: a man sitting on the sidewalk with matted hair, a threadbare t-shirt, and cardboard sign panhandling for money. Instinctively, I knew better, but you always think of Vegas as a tourist town, an escape, not a place where people are born and raised and live. As The Mirage drew closer, I tried to put it out of my brain and focus on what the hell I was about to get into.

As I entered the cavernous lobby, I tried to find my way to a desk where someone could assist me, but everyone looked busy with guests. As I lingered around one line of people, an employee appeared from a door behind the desk and, before she could aid her colleague with the guests, saw me craning my neck and looking around.

"Sir, can I help you?"

"Uh, yeah…I'm here to see David Blake," I offered, hopefully.

"Popular guy," she smiled.

"Oh?"

"Oh yes, Mr. Blake is a faithful guest of The Mirage, loves to entertain," she said with a smile.

"So, where do I…"

"Tower suite, all the way at the top," she nodded her head upwards as she said it.

I nodded back as if I knew what this meant and meandered toward the nearest bank of elevators. Miraculously, the first one to open for me emptied completely, and I found myself flying solo, pushing the highest number I saw. On the way up, I started to relax a bit, determined, at long last, to enjoy at least one night of this trip around other human beings.

When the elevator doors opened, I found myself wandering down a long, ornately decorated corridor. I could hear the thump of music behind the walls somewhere, growing louder as I walked. Suddenly, I heard the clacking of high heels on the tile floor. From around the corner up ahead, a young woman in a cocktail dress power-walked with her phone glued to her ear.

"Look, just fucking come pick me up, OK?!" she insisted to whoever was on the other end. After pausing to listen for a moment, she kicked off her heels in frustration, picked them up, and continued barefoot toward the elevators, giving me a curious glance as she passed. I turned the corner where she'd just emerged and saw some marble pillars along one of the walls framing a large door, behind which the music was blasting away. At a loss, I walked up, took a deep breath, and knocked loudly with my fist.

Moments later, the door opened, unleashing an increase in the music's volume that startled me. A stout, muscular guy with a razor bald head and goatee emerged and glared at me.

"Can I help you?" he asked with impatience. I had no clue what to say. After an awkward beat, I remembered the business card, fished it out of my pocket, and handed it to him.

"Where'd you get this?" he asked, glancing at the card then back to me.

"David gave it to me last Sunday, at Mandalay," I ventured, hoping this was, in fact, the right party.

"Stay right here," he commanded me before retreating inside the door and shutting it. I waited nervously for about two minutes before it opened again, revealing the doorman, who beckoned me in with a silent nod of his head.

I walked in, took one look around, and felt my body temperature change immediately.

The dim, fluorescent lighting, the music, the way people were standing, their gestures, their attire and, most of all, the looks they cast my way, all combined to give me a vibe not all that different from the vague feeling of dread on the plane; it was as if I'd just stumbled into a den of wolves whose sharp glare was helpfully informing me that I didn't belong. Before I could make any kind of move, David came through the crowd and saw me.

"Owen! Chicago in the house!" he bellowed, rushing over to give me a clumsy hug. He was miles from sober.

"Thanks for inviting me, this is quite the spread you have here," I yelled above the music.

"Yeah, this is my palace!" he shouted triumphantly.

"Who are these people?" I asked, glancing around at the thirty or so men and women mingling in the humongous suite with floor to ceiling windows looking out on the city.

"Friends, business partners, it's all good here. Work the room a little, you can probably put something together for yourself," he offered.

"Cool," I said, failing to sound it. I had no clue what he meant, but I was feeling worse and worse about the whole thing by the moment. I saw David start to reach into his pocket.

"Here, man. You look a little tense." He grabbed my hand pressed something into it. I opened my palm and saw two white circular pills. Ecstasy? I had no idea and just slipped them into my pocket.

"Oh, thanks," I said, trying to sound appreciative.

"Don't say I never did anything for ya!" he grinned before someone across the room caught his eye. "Listen, I gotta go talk to a guy about business. Enjoy yourself, man. Glad you made it!" He was walking past me before he even finished talking. I watched him make his way across the room before I found myself, again, on an island and unsure where to move.

Toward one corner of the suite, I saw an open door with a light on inside and thought it might be a bathroom, so I made my way toward it. Walking in, I found it was a large bathroom and saw a guy with shaggy black hair in a suit at the sink. I was never a drug person, but I didn't need to be to realize he was snorting cocaine off the counter with a rolled-up dollar bill. Upon my entrance, he looked a bit startled, then curiously gave me the once over. He nodded towards the remaining line of coke on the counter then offered the rolled-up dollar my way.

"First one's free," he said, friendly enough. I felt my pulse quicken again. Remembering the pills, I scooped them out of my pocket and displayed them as if they were some sort of currency.

"No, thanks, I'm all set," I said, managing a smile, which he returned.

"Cool," he replied, then snorted the line on the counter before giving me a polite nod on his way out.

As soon as he was gone, I went to the door, shut it and locked it. Alone, I finally exhaled a bit, but then wondered what I was going to do. I looked at the pills in my palm again. I could feel my heart pounding in my chest.

"Get the fuck out of here," I said aloud, as if the thought alone wouldn't be enough to convince me. I walked over to the toilet and flushed the pills, whatever they were. After another moment to gather myself, I unlocked the door, exited, and slinked along the wall of the suite, not drawing much attention. A minute later, I found myself face to face with the doorman again, this time on the inside. He raised an eyebrow at me, looking annoyed.

"I don't feel well," I said, not nearly loud enough for him to hear. I'm not sure if he read my lips, but he opened the door for me to leave, glaring again, probably still wondering who the hell I was.

Once out the door, I could still feel the dreadful urgency, as if the danger hadn't passed. I hurried to the elevators, watched the numbers impatiently light up as I headed downward, then bolted out the doors through the lobby.

Out on the crowded street, I walked as quickly as I could, bumping shoulders with a few people who gave me dirty looks as I hurried past. My legs were burning as I finally approached Mandalay. I wanted to get into my room as badly as I ever wanted to get back to my apartment after some ordinary or awkward social gathering.

I was practically jogging across the last street before the hotel and was already heading for the ground before I realized what I was tripping over. I braced myself with an outstretched hand, scraping it a bit on the pavement as I glanced back at the homeless man I'd seen on the way earlier, sprawled out and bewildered.

"Sorry!" I called out to him as I scrambled away toward the entrance to the hotel. The elevator ride took an eternity, but I finally made it to the thirty-first floor and sprinted down the hallway to the safe harbor of my room. I tried to calm myself down, feeling my breathing slow as I sat down on the edge of the bed.

As rattled as I was after rushing out of the party, my thoughts drifted back to the homeless man sitting on the sidewalk. I wanted to feel empathy for him in the same way I felt it for the people affected by the hurricanes, but even that brief pang of conscience failed to materialize. The numbness had set it. If I was honest with myself, it had been setting in for years.

I got up off the bed and walked over to the window. I wondered if choosing Vegas had been an inevitability. Where else would you go when the whole country seemed to be having a slow-rolling nervous breakdown? What else would you do but stand at the window of your room in a high-rise hotel and stare through your reflection at this preposterous neon bulb of a city in the middle of an ancient desert, unable to tell where the lights stopped and the darkness began?

I walked over to the desk, pulled my notebook out of my bag, sat down, and began to write. I started with the day I'd handed my vacation papers to Joel at One World and worked my way forward, almost like a diary of how I had got from there to here. It didn't have much structure or flow, but it felt cathartic to get it on paper. As the sun started to rise over the desert, over my last full day in Vegas, I collapsed onto my bed and slept like a baby.

This time, I knew right where I was.

I woke up in mid-afternoon, starving for a meal. I pulled myself together and decided I'd pay one last visit to the hole-in-the-wall for a burger and fries. Once there, I took my time and enjoyed the meal as much as I could, already fretting over the frantic day of travel ahead of me tomorrow. I'd have to get up early to make it to the airport in time, and I knew that anxiety would persist until I touched down in Chicago, making a note to myself to call Alex about getting a ride home.

As I walked back to the hotel, I could see and hear the commotion over at the festival, its last night already in full swing. My sleep schedule being altered again, I planned on going back up to my room, getting a drink or two out of the mini-bar, and relaxing by the window as the festival reached its crescendo. On the way up, I found myself in the elevator with a heavy-set guy with a goatee wearing a t-shirt with a logo on it for 95.5 The Bull, which I assumed was the country music station of choice in Vegas.

"Checking out the festival tonight?" he asked in a great radio voice.

"No," I sighed, "Country just isn't my style."

"That doesn't matter, you can still go have fun. I cover these festivals all over the country and this one is a blast!"

The elevator stopped and we were joined by a middle-aged husband and wife before we continued our ascent.

"I'm headed back up to my room to get some equipment. I have a few extra passes from the radio station. Free of charge. You sure you don't want one?" he asked. He was so friendly, I felt bad for refusing, but after the night before, I just wanted to be alone.

"Thanks for offering, but I fly out tomorrow morning. Just want to get some sleep," I explained. The husband and wife turned to us.

"You have tickets to the festival?" the wife asked, obviously excited.

"Sure, you guys wanna go?" the DJ responded, as if they were old pals.

"Oh, I'd just love to see Jason Aldean!" the wife beamed. The husband chuckled and rolled his eyes. "She loves him almost as much as me," he informed us. I smiled, the DJ laughed.

"I'm on 33, I'll be about fifteen minutes. You guys meet me back down in the lobby and I'll have the passes then, OK?" At this, the wife seemed as if she might do a happy dance and, as the elevator let me off at 31, she excitedly told her husband she couldn't believe their luck.

I walked back to my room, got my things organized and sat my suitcase and shoulder bag by the doors. In the morning, I'd just have to shower, get changed, and I'd be gone. Alex's question rang in my mind. Now what?

Reclining on the bed with a beer, I watched some of the Sunday night NFL game and scrolled through Facebook on my phone for the first time all trip. I almost never posted—had little to post—and didn't feel compelled to share vapid memes and videos with anyone. I hadn't even taken a picture since I'd arrived.

The Seahawks were blowing out the Colts, so I aimlessly surfed through the channels as night settled in outside and the lights from the festival started to fill up my window panes.

Around ten, I was startled by a series of loud bangs from somewhere above me in the hotel. Glancing up at the ceiling, I thought maybe there was construction going on in the building, but it seemed late at night for such work to be in progress. A few minutes later, there was another loud noise, something like dishes crashing to the floor and I wondered if someone had spilled a room service cart. Straining my ear, I then heard a series of faint popping sounds, not unlike fireworks going off. I got up and walked to the window, expecting to see some pyrotechnic display going on at the festival.

I looked down into chaos. People were running every direction, bouncing into and off each other in a manic game of human pinball. My heart jumped. What the hell was going on? I focused on two young women who seemed as if they didn't know where to go, one grabbing the other's hand and practically dragging her along. The moment after my eyes settled on the girl being pulled, she was propelled violently forward and fell lifeless to the ground, landing with her limbs in an awkward tangle.

Gunshots.

Someone was shooting from somewhere nearby. I stood at the window, frozen in place, not looking at anything in particular, beholding the panic in total. Maybe thirty seconds passed, maybe ten minutes.

There was more noise from up above, I glanced upward, thinking about what those sounds could have been and feeling the color drain from my cheeks. Was someone shooting from the hotel? Multiple shooters? A terrorist attack? Was a bomb about to go off? Were bullets about to rip through my wall? I was terrified by the pure possibility of the moment.

I found myself glancing nervously around the room, pacing between the bed and the window. My instinct was to run somewhere, anywhere. I wanted so badly to be with other people, to feel anything resembling solidarity, even if it was in unbridled fear. I wanted out, but the next thing I did was run to my door and make sure it was locked. I started to walk back to the window, then hesitated. Grabbing the remote off the bed, I turned the channel to CNN. A commercial for soap. I hurriedly located the viewing guide on the desk and turned it to a local channel. A blood-red banner was splashed across the bottom of the screen: REPORT: SHOTS FIRED AT MUSIC FESTIVAL.

I sat down on the edge of the bed and watched as the anchors seemed, like me, to have far more questions than answers. They were showing hastily recorded footage on a loop, a blur of lights and screams set against darkness, someone running for their life after they'd pressed the button. I switched the channel back to CNN and what looked to be the same video was running above a similar red banner on the bottom of the screen. I probably knew more than they did.

The phone on the nightstand rang, about knocking me off the bed. Scrambling over to answer it, I heard a recorded message playing: "An emergency has been reported in the hotel. All guests are requested to shelter in place. Police are responding. This is not a drill." I listened to the message repeat several times, still trying to grasp that this was really happening, wanting this voice recorded months or years prior to speak specifically to me, to tell me it was going to be alright.

Hanging up the room phone, I reached for my cell. It was after midnight back in Illinois. Alex would be asleep. So would my mom. These thoughts triggered a realization that I was going to have to tell this story to them, to everyone.

Everyone was going to want to know what happened. It made me feel ill but, at that moment, I needed to talk to someone.

Dad. He lives in the same time zone.

I quickly found his number in my contacts for the first time in months—maybe even a year—and he answered on the second ring. I wondered if he still had me in his phone.

"Hello?"

"Dad…" Where to begin?

"Owen? Are you there?"

"Yeah, it's me, dad. Are you near a TV?"

"Um, yeah, I'm home, why?"

"Turn on CNN." I could tell he was confused, and there was a beat of silence as he absorbed this strange request.

"Maya, turn on CNN," I heard him instruct his wife, a woman I'd met just twice.

"What?" I heard her voice in the background.

"Just do it!" dad insisted. A moment later, the change had apparently been made.

"Jesus, another mass shooting?!" he exclaimed.

"Dad, I'm there. I'm in Vegas."

"My god, Owen, are you OK?! Where are you?"

"I'm in my hotel room, I'm OK."

"Which hotel?"

"Mandalay. I think the shooting is coming from here."

He exhaled sharply before speaking. "Jesus...Owen is out there in Vegas!" he said, apparently to Maya. "Owen, is your room locked?"

"I think so, let me make sure." I knew it was, but I wanted to make him feel as if he'd reminded me to do it for some reason.

"It's locked," I confirmed.

"OK, my god, Owen, I'm up and pacing around here, I can't believe this..." he trailed off.

"I know, dad. I'm scared," my voice was barely above a whisper.

"You're gonna be fine, Owen," he responded instantly, perhaps instinctively, "Just stay in your room and don't open the door unless you know it's the police, OK?"

He wasn't telling me anything different than the recorded message from the hotel, but it felt reassuring to hear it from him.

"OK...I just needed to talk to someone."

"You're there alone? What are you doing out in Vegas?" he asked, the mood of the conversation lightening just a bit.

"Just on vacation. And yeah, I'm by myself."

"Oh. Have you called your mother?"

"No. Too late back east."

"Yeah, that's true. Have you talked to her lately?"

"Um, no, it's been awhile, I guess."

There was a long moment of silence. I wasn't sure what to say next.

"Owen…" he started, then paused. In the brief silence, I heard another prolonged burst of gunfire, the muffled popping sounds resembling some kind of monster breathing underwater.

"Yeah?"

"I don't know why I'm saying this now, but I just want you to know how much I love you. And I'm so sorry we had to put you through what we did right when you were getting ready to get out on your own. I just…" he sounded as if he couldn't find the words.

"I love you, too," I said, feeling a choking sensation in my throat. I heard him take a deep breath.

"I just want you to be OK."

"I will be, dad. Thank you…I'm gonna go now, dad," I informed him. I wanted to keep talking, to catch up, but I was a wreck and felt like I might burst into tears.

"Call me back if you need to talk. If you need anything, Owen."

"OK…bye." I hung up and laid back on the bed, feeling a surprising safety in that simple act.

There was a loud knocking at the door.

"Police! Open up!"

I leaped to my feet and hurried to the door, squinting the through the peephole at a man in a dark suit holding up his badge and three uniformed officers in tactical gear.

"Open up!" the voice insisted again, "We need to clear this room!"

I took a deep breath and unlocked the door. As soon as it was open, the man in the suit took me by the arm and escorted me out into the hallway, clearing the way for the officers to pour in, guns drawn.

"Come with me," he said, pulling me along for the first few steps as we walked, his other hand never far from the gun holstered on his hip. We turned a corner and I saw another team of police at the end of the hallway, clearing another room. "I'm Detective Ventura, Las Vegas PD," he informed, "We're clearing all the guests on this floor and taking them down to 28."

We rounded a corner to the area where the elevators were. There were four or five other frightened guests there. He nodded toward them after pushing the call button. "There will be someone from our department there when you get off," he said to all of us, turning to hustle back down the hallway almost before he'd finished speaking. It was all happening so fast, I couldn't speak. As we piled into the elevator, I looked at a lady holding her young son, no more than five years old. As the elevator took the quick trip down to 28, I made eye contact with him over his mother's shoulder. He had been crying and looked so afraid. Me, too, buddy.

I'd been sitting with dozens of other guests in the hallway for what seemed like eternity. People were crying, speaking in hushed tones, texting furiously. I was finally around other people, but now had no desire—or ability, seemingly—to speak to them. I glanced down at my scraped hand and grimaced at the sight of anything resembling blood. Detectives and officers had been hustling past, a few stopping to assure us everything was under control. As I stared at the carpet, elbows on my knees, I heard a loud voice.

"Folks, everything is going to be OK. There's no more immediate threat. We'll be releasing you back to your rooms soon. Just sit tight," it was Detective Ventura again, still all business. A few minutes later, he escorted me and about six others back up to 31. I glanced down at my watch. It was after one in the morning. When we got off the elevator, Detective Ventura addressed us.

"We're going to need you all to stay in your rooms tonight. Officers will be posted on each floor for your protection. If you need anything, call the lobby." He paused a moment before continuing. "If you need to talk to someone, we'll have grief counselors here in the morning. Come to the main lobby and we'll do everything we can to help you. For now, just know that we're doing our best and the hotel has been secured." His face was a mixture of intense concentration and sadness. This was a man, I thought, who had seen death up close for years.

Everyone walked back to their rooms, mostly in silence. I still hadn't spoken since I ended my call with my dad. Back in my room, I noticed that the sheets were messed up a bit and the contents of the desk were scattered from where they'd been, but otherwise, the room was as I left it. Finally, I walked back over to the window and looked down. There were so many police cars and emergency vehicles down below, it was hard to see anything in the sea of colored lights, as if the usual glow of Vegas had been amplified to somehow be even brighter. The TV was still on CNN. I turned and looked at the screen long enough to see the word "casualties" and then turned away, thinking of the young woman I'd seen shot down.

I decided to take a hot shower, sitting on the floor of the tub and letting the water cascade over me. I must have been in a long time because I didn't stand back up until I felt the water turn lukewarm on my skin. After drying off, I got dressed and grabbed my phone. It was getting towards first light back in Chicago. I opened my conversation with Alex and sent him a text:

"hey man, just wanted u to know I'm OK"

I wanted to write so much more but couldn't make sense of it all at that moment, so I hit send. Then I thought of my mom. I knew I'd have to tell her eventually, but I didn't want her to worry. I had some days left on my vacation. Maybe I could see her. I'd text her later that morning, I decided.

No room service this morning. Instead, I laid in bed and watched TV, consciously avoiding news but thinking about how the rest of the nation, no doubt, was waking up and learning about the shooting.

I dozed off and found myself on the Strip, within the police perimeter, flat on my back. Glancing to the left, I saw a white sheet draped over a prone body. To my right, there was an older man lying lifeless, eyes still open, with blood smeared on his cheek. A pair of hands appeared, draping a white sheet over him. A moment later, the same sterile whiteness enveloped me.

My eyes were opening. It was time to wake up.

Seeing the time, I knew I had to get moving soon if I wanted to make it to the airport, which prompted me to wonder if they were even going to let us leave the hotel. Did the cops want to talk to me again? Was the airport even open? I had no clue but gathered up my things and prepared to head down for checkout. Before exiting the room, I couldn't resist turning the channel to CNN just for a minute.

After a commercial ended, another video taken from a smartphone was aired. Whoever was holding the phone kept it remarkably stable as it captured a bunch of festival-goers crouching down in fear. Except for one. I actually laughed as I saw one young guy, tank top, beer in hand, standing defiantly as people repeatedly shouted, "Get down!" Looking unfazed, he casually raised his non-drinking hand and extended his middle finger in what he felt was the shooter's general vicinity. In the wake of such tragedy, it was oddly refreshing to see someone stare down this violent absurdity and tell it to go fuck itself. Down in the corner of the screen, I noticed the time again and finally turned off the TV before exiting the room and heading down to the lobby.

What a change.

This space that had been so bustling and loud with laughter all week now felt like a tomb. There were people huddled on couches, conversing in hushed tones. Parents held their frightened children close. I noticed a handful of people moving between the different groupings, remembering Detective Ventura's remark about grief counselors. The night before, I'd wanted to talk to someone but wasn't able, now I was able to speak but didn't particularly want to. Shit, I thought again, I'm going to have to tell this story to everyone, eventually. Mom, Alex, everyone at One World, everyone whom I might one day meet who would learn that I was here for this. I would no longer just be Owen Miller to them, I'd also be Mass Shooting Survivor Guy and I was dreading it already.

I started walking towards the nearest desk until I passed a couch where an older woman was sitting alone. I slowed as I felt a jolt of recognition: it was my silent neighbor from the plane ride out. With a blank expression, she stood up as I walked by, almost as if she didn't see me; I stopped a moment before we would have collided. I let go of the handle on my suitcase and put my hand out instinctively as if to ask if she was OK. Her face and body language spoke of a sadness so deep it was inexpressible. Without warning, she threw her arms around me, embracing me tightly as she started to cry. I felt her chest heaving, heard her uneven gasps between sobs, felt the dampness of tears against the side of my neck where her face was resting. Slowly, I put my arms around her. Had she lost a child? A grandchild? Her spouse? The possibility suddenly had me on the verge of tears when I'd been laughing at the TV screen minutes earlier. I was a mess. It was all a mess.

"It's going to be OK," I said aloud, as much to myself as to her. She released the hug and made eye contact with me. I saw the faintest of smiles form before she reassuringly squeezed my shoulders and walked away without a word.

After watching her walk toward the elevators for a moment, I turned and gathered myself enough to complete my walk over to the desk. A young hotel employee came over and asked if I was checking out. When I said yes, he informed me that the front entrances to the hotel were closed off and I'd have to take another route and leave via the parking garages. He punched a few keys on the computer, then printed out a copy of my bill and slid it in front of me. The room service and mini-bar charges made me cringe but, at the moment, it was easy to get over. I signed and paid with my credit card, then awkwardly wandered around the lobby, following signage directing me to the parking garages. As I walked, I pulled out my phone and ordered an Uber to pick me up. Emerging from the darkness of the garage into the bright morning, I only had to wait a minute or two before a car pulled over to the curb.

"Owen?" the woman at the wheel asked. I nodded silently and climbed into the backseat. She didn't say a word on the drive to McCarran, a decision she probably made for everyone she picked up that day.

The airport was, in fact, open for business, and seemed like it was busy as ever. Once I got through security and checked my bag, I found my way to the waiting area near my gate and sat down with my shoulder bag in the seat next to me. I thought of the pages in my notebook. When I got back to Peoria, I was going to expand on it, I told myself. Maybe I finally had a story to tell. Before I could write it out, though, I needed to talk about it. Pulling my phone back out, I texted my mom:

"hey mom"

"hi baby! How are you?"

"Im OK, on vacation this week, actually, was wondering if I could come up and see you"

"Of course, that would be great! When were you thinking?"

"I can prob be there tonight by dinner"

"Sure thing! I'll be home from the store around 5"

"Cool, I'll let you know when I'm close"

"OK. Can't wait! Love you!"

I figured I could stay at her place for a day or two and try, somehow, to talk about what I'd been through before finding a way back to Peoria so I could decompress for a few days before returning to work.

Looking over at the bar area to my right, two flat screens were tuned to different news networks and each was focusing on the shooting. The banner at the bottom of one screen read, "Tipping Point For Gun Control?" with a handful of people in discussion, the other showed a reporter live from Vegas with the caption, "Police Searching For Answers." The empty rituals had begun, a dance we'd done often enough to know the steps by heart: the debates would be furious on social media, formulaic in the halls of power, then the numbness would set in and nothing would happen, the nation long since having decided constant tragedy was more bearable than substantive change.

Scrolling across the bottom of one screen, I saw the body count, far worse even than I'd imagined. Dozens dead, hundreds wounded. I thought of the DJ and the couple in the elevator. Were they OK? Wounded? Dead? I'd probably never know and decided it was better that way. One of the TV's was now showing a live exterior shot of Mandalay. Amid the giant mirror of windows reflecting the morning sun, one broken pane was eerily covered with a tarp billowing in the breeze. I wasn't sure which window was my room, but I couldn't have been more than two hundred feet from where the bullets were escaping the gun. I thought of the shooter. I knew his picture would soon be staring out at me from every TV screen and newspaper and I'd wonder if I'd seen him in the hotel, shared an elevator ride, or brushed past him in the hallway by chance. The next thought to pass through my head was bizarrely American, that something as trivial as my taste in music may have spared me from being brutally murdered in a mass shooting. It really was strange to be alive right now, but I was walking back into my life with the knowledge that I somehow possessed the dumb luck required to survive this ruthless new century.

My phone vibrated in my pocket as I was getting on the plane and I took it out as soon as I sat down. It was a text from Alex:

"holy shit dude I just saw the news! Fucking crazy world man. So glad to hear ur OK, have so many questions for you but I'm sure u will tell me all about it. Flying back today? Need a ride just let me know"

"Thanks but I won't need a ride, going to stay w/mom in the city for a few days"

That was all I could muster at the moment, plus a flight attendant was instructing me over the P.A. to switch my phone off or to airplane mode, with me then doing the latter. I tried to get comfortable and felt a wave of sleepiness wash over me.

"Mr. Miller?" I heard a pleasant voice ask. Looking up, I saw a flight attendant standing in the aisle, towering over me.

"Yeah?" I said, wondering what was going on.

"Come with me, you've been upgraded."

"Oh…" I lingered for a moment before what she'd said could sink in. Still baffled, I stood, picked up my shoulder bag, and followed her toward the front of the coach cabin. Was this the airline? The hotel? I hadn't a clue and was too weary to care much more about it.

She led me through a door and into the first-class cabin, where I was directed to a large cushioned seat with a wooden table extending out in front of it, upon which I plopped my bag as I sat down and stretched out. I may have had a ton of post-traumatic stress to deal with, but at least I'd have plenty of leg room.

A few minutes later, the plane took off without me experiencing the anxiety I normally had. There was a new anxiety to replace it. Namely, that feeling of sadness that followed the end of a vacation, this time multiplied by a few million. As we reached our cruising altitude, I considered what I was coming back to. I could no longer bullshit my way around the fact that my life was incredibly empty and lonely. I thought back to the night before and those panicked moments after the shooting started, those moments when I'd wanted to be anything but alone, alone like I'd been in my apartment for years, like I'd be when I got back to Peoria. I replayed the phone call with dad. As my mind drifted, I found myself thinking, and desirously so, of so many things that I'd been hiding from for so long. I told myself I'd never want or need these things, but I finally admitted I did. I wanted the friends, and the social life, and the let's meet for drinks after work. I wanted to fall in love, to remember feeling vulnerable could be a good thing. I wanted the wife and the kids and the daddy you're so silly and the laughing in bed on Sunday mornings.

Maybe I was experiencing some type of euphoria that follows a trauma. Maybe I didn't have a clue how to pursue those things. For now, I was content to just recline and ponder the possibilities as we hurtled our way through the jet stream, east to the future.

Considering the twenty-four hours I'd had, the tumult of Midway was nothing to trouble me. I sent a text to mom, telling her I could be in the suburbs in an hour or so. Walking out to the curb lane, I ordered an Uber and sat on my suitcase, waiting. Eventually, an SUV pulled up to collect me. Once I settled into the backseat, my driver confirmed my destination before pulling away and, for some reason, I fixated on the trinkets hanging from his rear-view mirror as they swayed back and forth. After we got out onto the street, his attempt at small talk commenced.

"Where you fly in from, man?" he asked, a slight Caribbean accent to his voice.

"Vegas," I blurted before I could consider some white lie.

He focused on a wide left turn through a busy intersection for a moment before eventually coming to a stop in a line of traffic.

"Vegas, huh?" he asked, intrigued. Here it comes, I thought. Then he asked me a question, just not the one I had expected.

"So, did you win big?"

Acknowledgments

Thank you to Unsolicited Press for believing in me and letting me tell my story. I'm also grateful to my friends and family who have supported and encouraged me through the years (and indulged my need for constant feedback). In particular, I'm indebted to Ben Davis, who listened when no one else would, and Shawn Van Horn, for being an honest editor and a loyal friend. Lastly, and most importantly, thanks and love to Lindsay, who changed my life, and to Clara, who makes each day beautiful.

Bibliography

Fight Club. Directed by David Fincher. Screenplay by Jim Uhls. United States: 20th Century Fox, 1999. DVD.

Heaney, Seamus. *Station Island.* 1st ed. London: Faber and Faber, 1984.

Kerouac, Jack. *On the Road.* New York: Viking Press, 1957.

Office Space. Directed by Mike Judge. Screenplay by Mike Judge. United States: 20th Century Fox, 1999. DVD.

Thompson, Hunter S. *Fear and Loathing in Las Vegas: A Savage Journey to the Heart of the American Dream.* New York: Random House, 1971.

Thompson, Hunter S. *Hells Angels: The Strange and Terrible Saga of the Outlaw Motorcycle Gangs.* New York: Random House, 1966.

About the Author

Adam Gibbs is a writer and poet from Grove City, Ohio. His poetry has appeared in *Fourth and Sycamore*, *The Mark Literary Review*, and been honored by the Hayner Cultural Center and Tipp City Arts Council. He lives with his wife Lindsay and their daughter Clara.

About the Press

Unsolicited Press is based in Portland, Oregon. The team produces fiction, nonfiction, and poetry from emerging and award-winning authors.

Learn more at unsolicitedpress.com